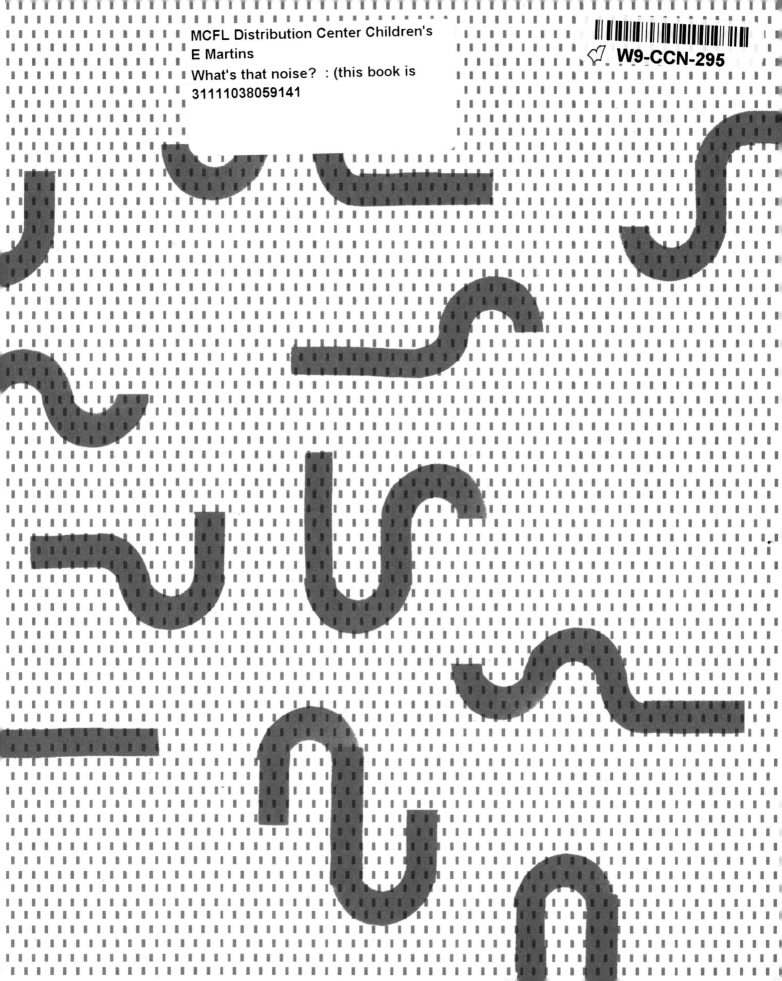

WHAT'S

First published 2016 by order of the Tate Trustees
by Tate Publishing, a division of Tate Enterprises Ltd,
Millbank, London SW1P 4RG
www.tate.org.uk/publishing

First published in Portuguese as *Este livro está a chamar-te. (Não ouves?)*
© Planeta Tangerina, Isabel Minhós Martins and Madalena Matoso 2013
English language edition © 2016 Tate Enterprises Ltd
Translated by Isabel Alves and Bergen Peck

A catalogue record for this book is available from the British Library
ISBN 978 1 84976 429 2

Distributed in the United States and Canada by ABRAMS, New York

Library of Congress Control Number applied for

Designed by Planeta Tangerina
Printed and bound in Portugal by Printer Portuguesa

THAT NOISE?

Isabel Minhós Martins
Madalena Matoso

(THIS BOOK IS CALLING YOU...)

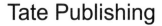

Tate Publishing

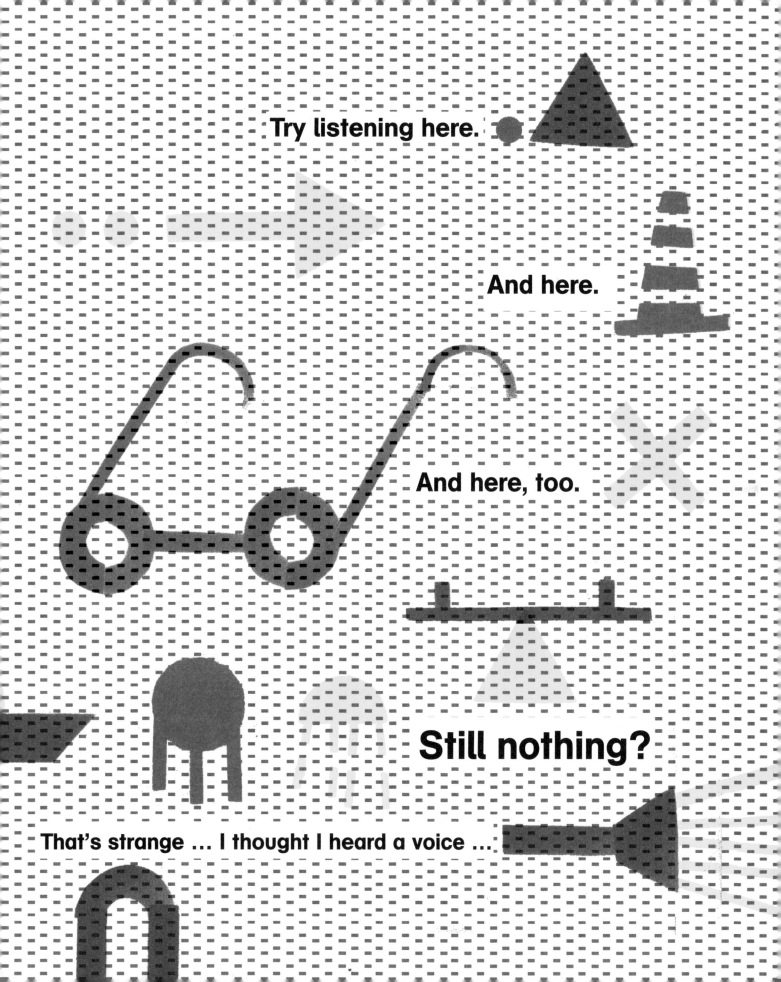

Put one hand here.

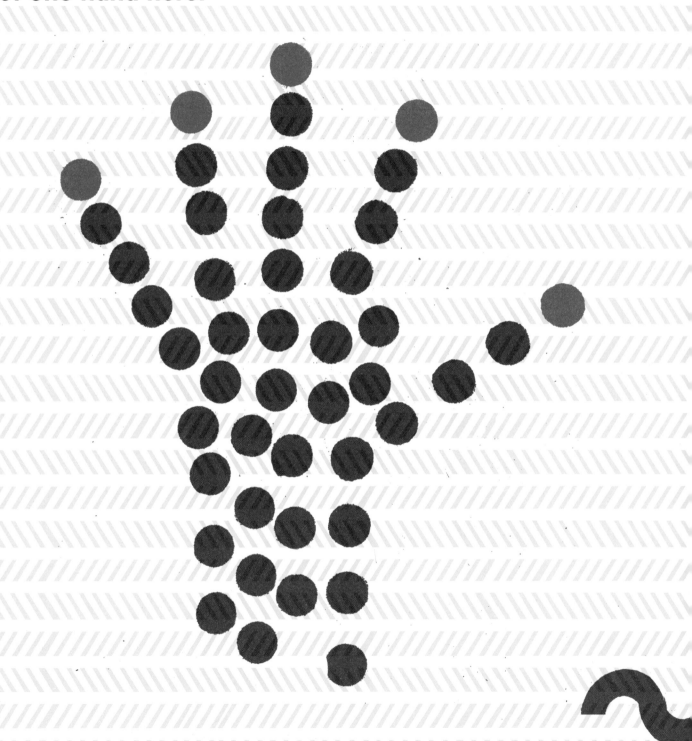

And the other one here.

(Well then: are they big or small?)

To tell this story
we'll need
your fingers,
your eyes,
your ears …
and maybe your nose …

Are you ready?
If so, patter your
fingers on the page
like a drum roll:
let the adventure begin!

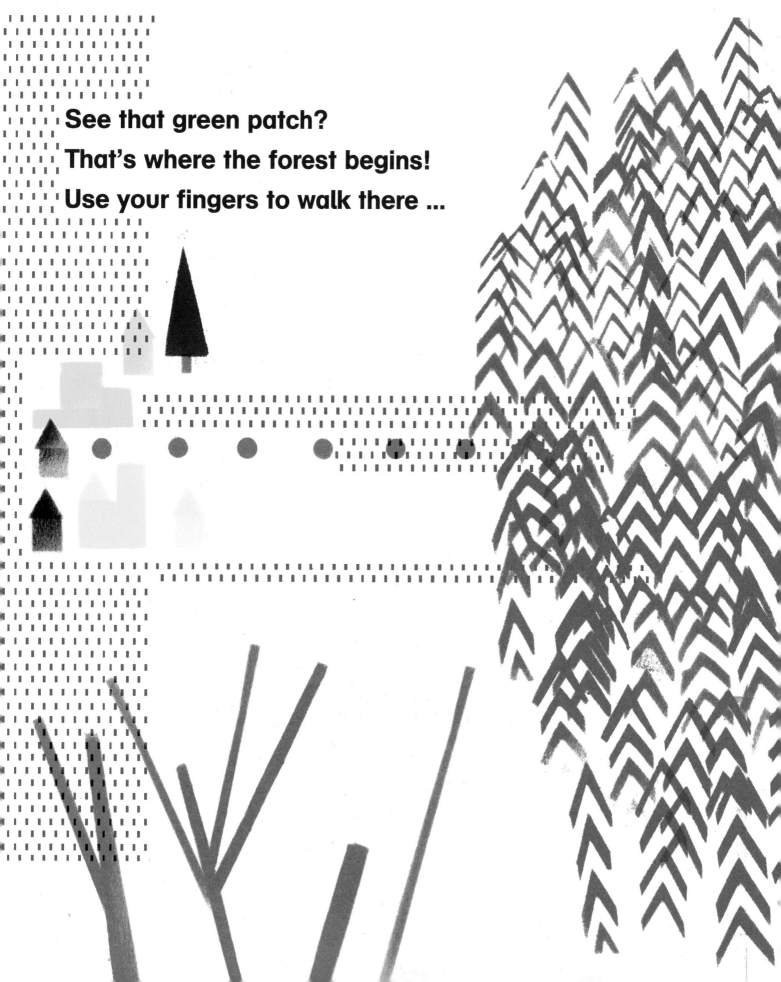

See that green patch?
That's where the forest begins!
Use your fingers to walk there ...

You've been very brave, but now hush ...
We're in an unknown forest, and we
don't know what dangers
might be lurking nearby ...

What's that noise?
Did you hear it?
(So did I, so did I ...)

It was that voice calling you, wasn't it?
I think it came from the next page ...
Turn it over carefully.
(You're not afraid of animals, are you?)

oh!

Look at the leaves, they've been eaten ...

Look at the trail left on the ground ...

There was something here,

but it seems to have run away!

Follow the trail on tiptoe.

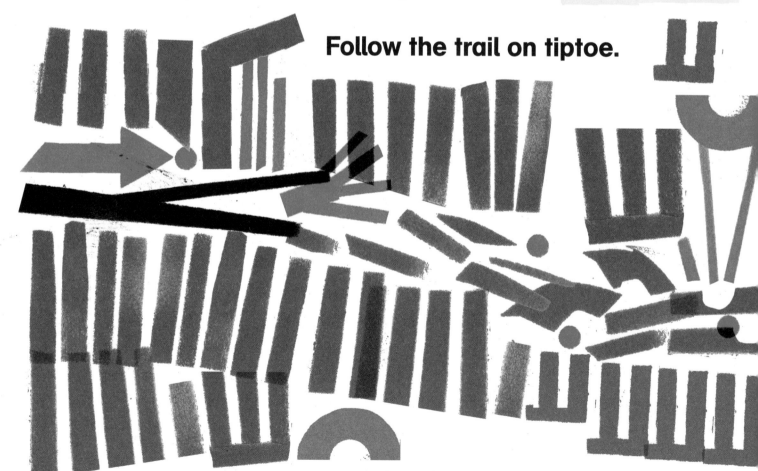

Look!
We've come
to a river.
What now?

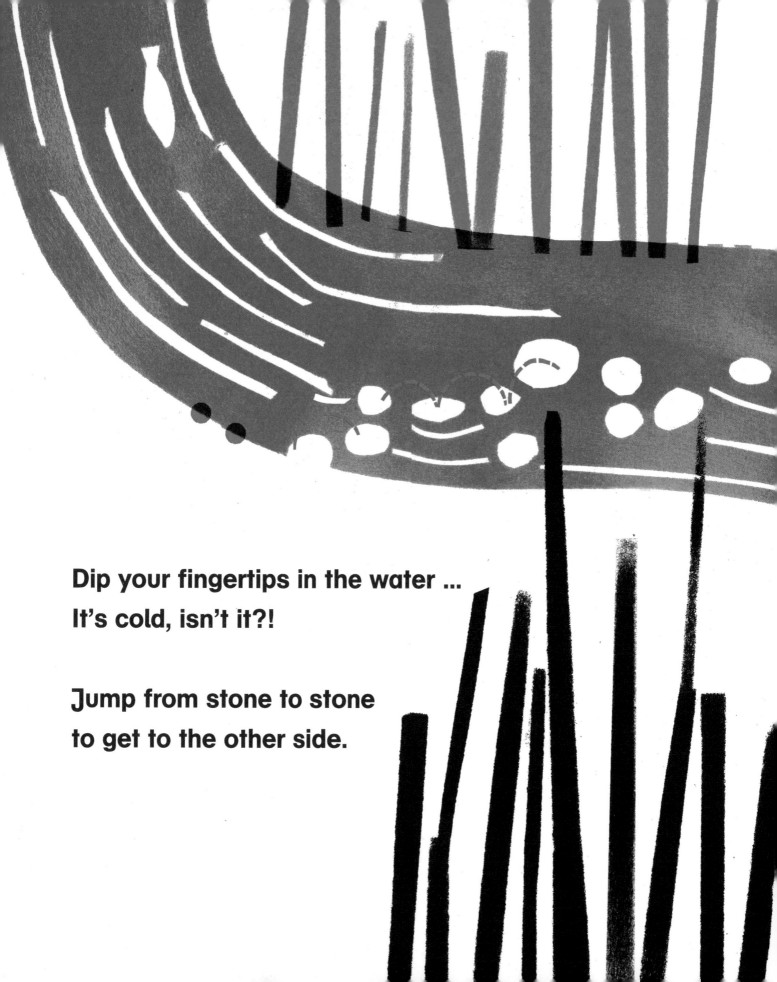

Dip your fingertips in the water ...
It's cold, isn't it?!

Jump from stone to stone
to get to the other side.

We made it!

Oh, it's starting
to rain!
(But it's only a few
small drops …
You will go on,
won't you?)

The drizzle has turned into a downpour, after all!
Touch the raindrops with your fingertips
to hear the sound of the rain:

slowly ...

stronger ...

a storm!

Run for shelter on the other side of this giant rock!

Phew!

It seems to have passed ...

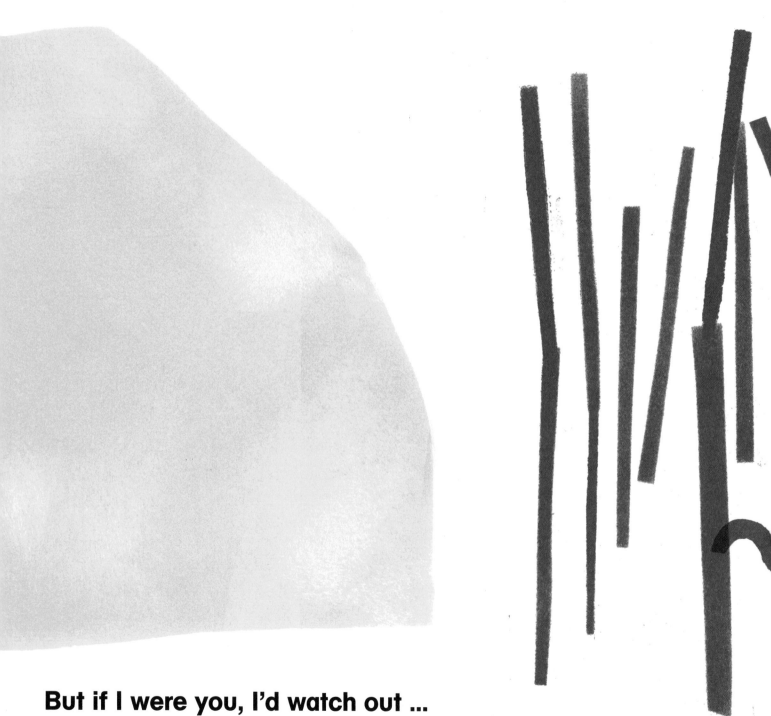

But if I were you, I'd watch out ...
Can you hear the grass move? It's moving and calling out ...

Who could it be?

Looks like they're playing hide and seek ...

OOPS!

It's gone again.
But this time
it's left us something ...
Something round and red.

What could it be?

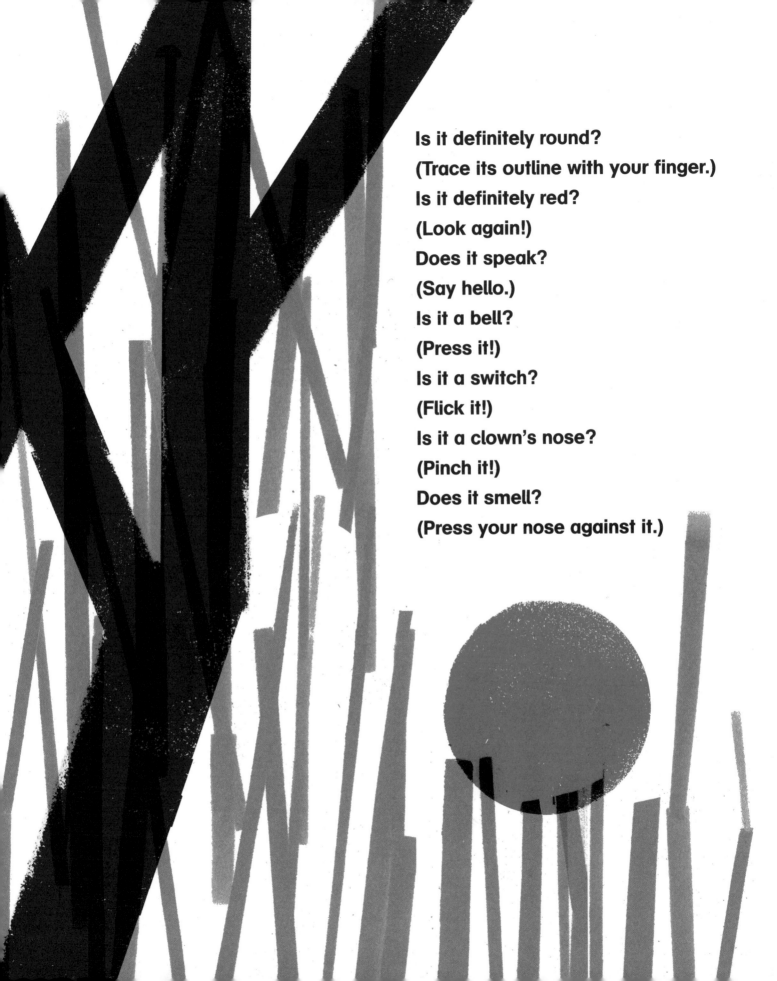

Is it definitely round?
(Trace its outline with your finger.)
Is it definitely red?
(Look again!)
Does it speak?
(Say hello.)
Is it a bell?
(Press it!)
Is it a switch?
(Flick it!)
Is it a clown's nose?
(Pinch it!)
Does it smell?
(Press your nose against it.)

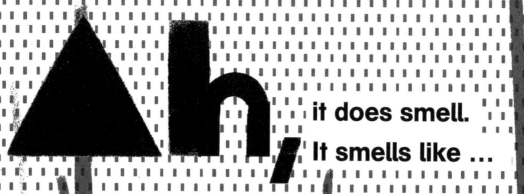

it does smell.

It smells like ...

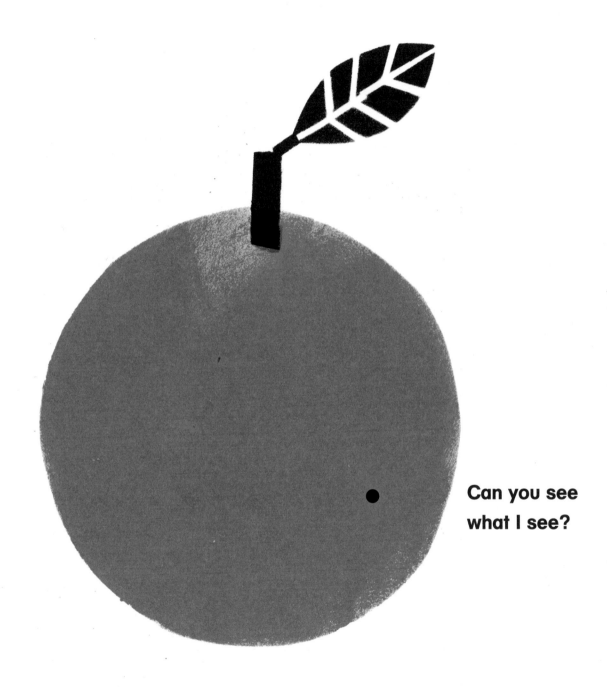

Can you see
what I see?

Take a peek.
(Step inside, but when you turn the page, don't open the book
too wide, or you'll let in too much light at once, OK?)

Oh! It's so dark.

Oh! There's someone in here.

(Make a frightened heartbeat with your fingers.)

We'd better get out of here.
I don't think it likes us invading its space ...

Now what shall we do?

Hasn't it realised yet that
we just want to be friends?

I know!

Let's show it there are no dangers out here.

I know!

Let's give it a present!

If it likes round, red things, maybe we should give it something round and red. Any ideas?

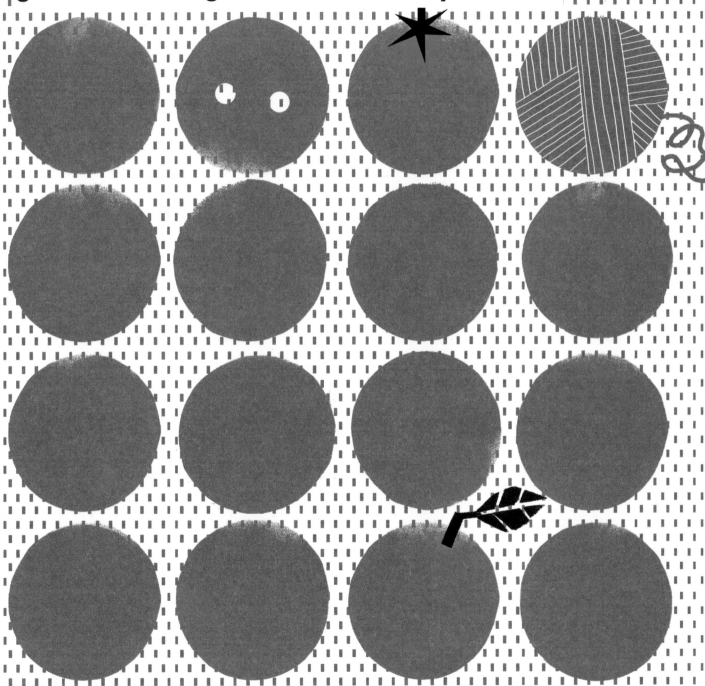

Run your fingers over the apple skin and call softly: "Come and see – I have something for you!"

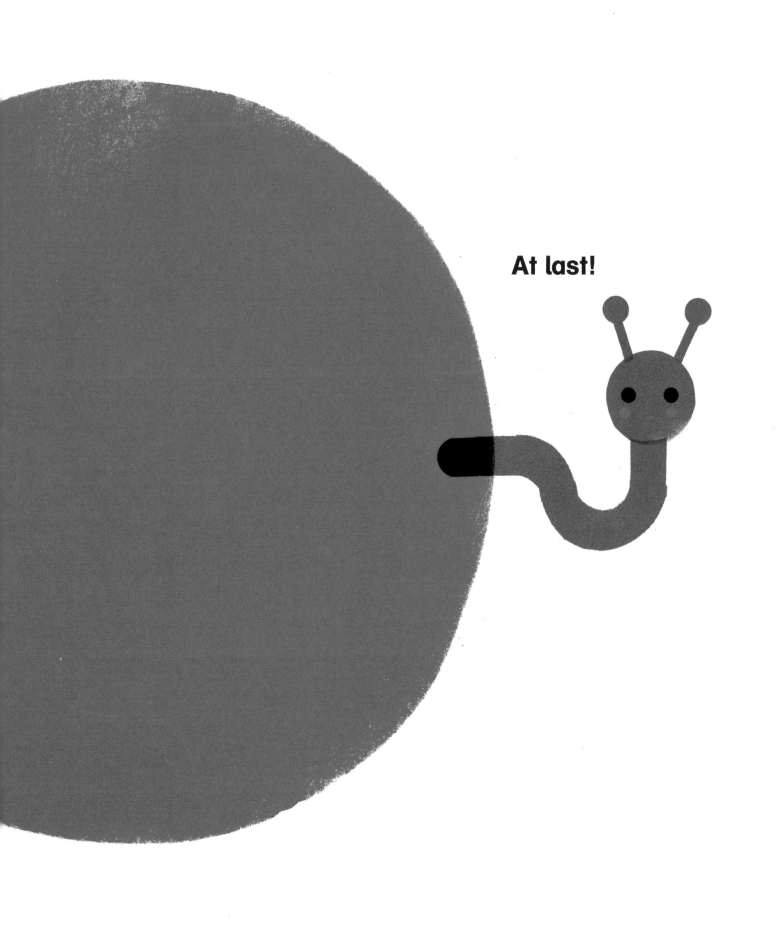

At last!

Take it easy, don't rush.
Make a worm with your finger
and slowly edge your way closer ...

There's so much to show your new friend!
Why don't you take it to the big rock in the creek
where you like to dive?

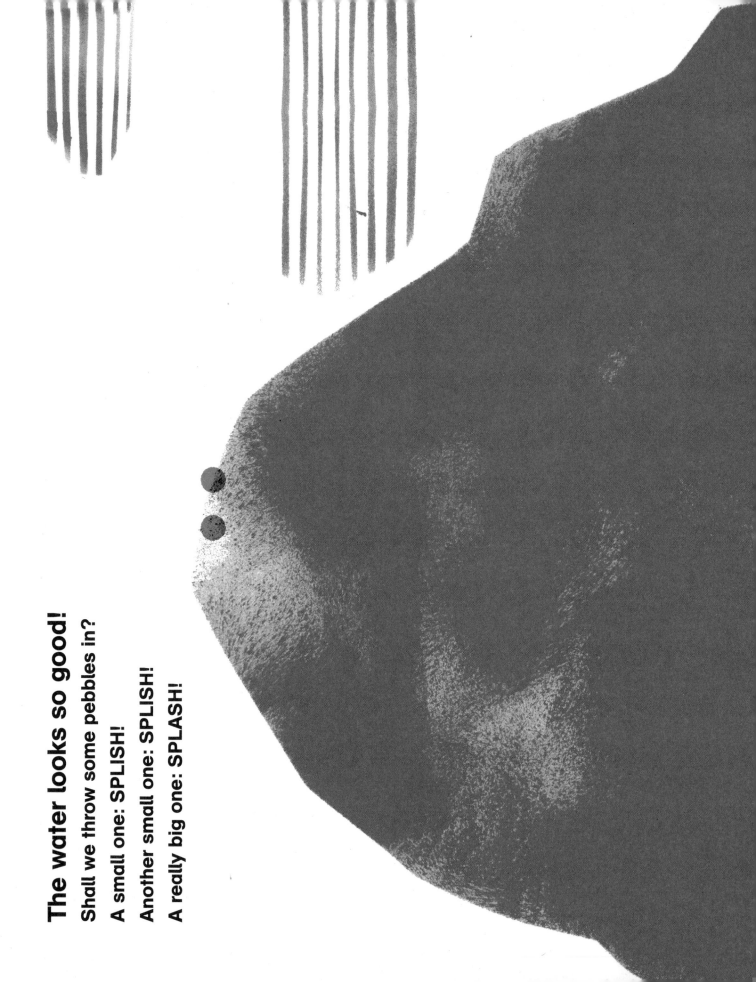

The water looks so good!

Shall we throw some pebbles in?

A small one: SPLISH!

Another small one: SPLISH!

A really big one: SPLASH!

Your turn now: 1, 2, 3 ... JUMP!

The grass is so soft.

The sun is so warm.

And a summer breeze is blowing ...

If you lie down, you and your new friend will be dry in no time!

Blow on the page softly to create a gentle breeze ...

**But what is this shadow
all of a sudden?**

It's a blackbird who has spotted the worm for its dinner!

Hurry, you must protect your friend!

Shelter it with the palm of your hand.

Phew, it's gone ...
There are some dangers out here after all!
But when you have a friend
by your side, everything is fine ...

See how happy it looks!

Make your hands into a round apple

for your worm friend to take shelter in.

Take a peek and see how it's sleeping, all nicely curled up ...

See you tomorrow.
(When the worm wakes up, it'll be delighted to see you.
Don't forget to come and see it once in a while!).

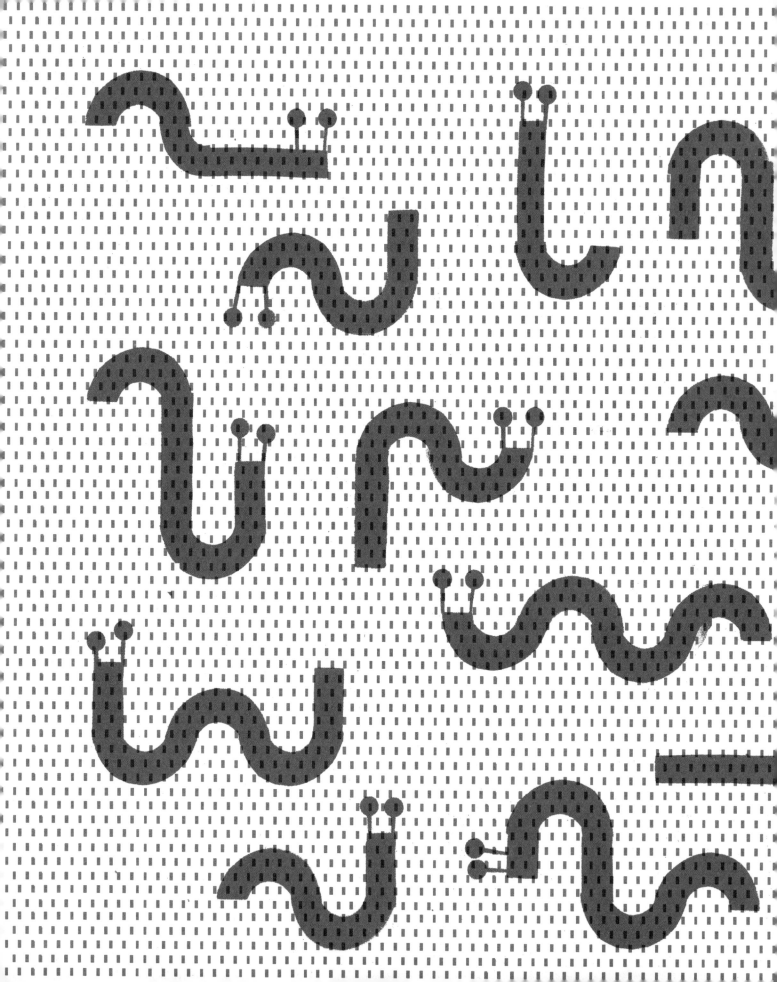